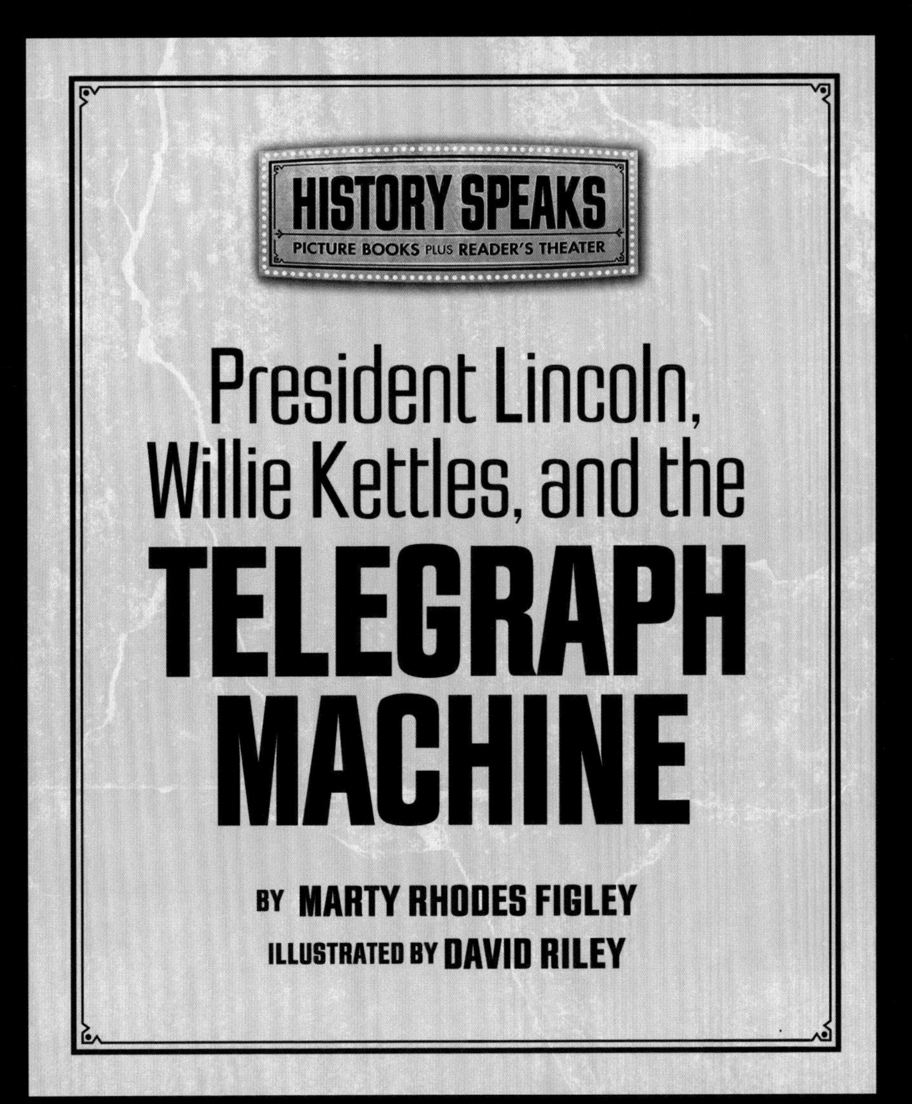

HISTORY SPEAKS

PICTURE BOOKS PLUS READER'S THEATER

President Lincoln, Willie Kettles, and the TELEGRAPH MACHINE

BY **MARTY RHODES FIGLEY**

ILLUSTRATED BY **DAVID RILEY**

MILLBROOK PRESS / MINNEAPOLIS

For my father, Robert C. Rhodes, to celebrate his love of history and his pioneering efforts in another type of communication, cable television —MRF

For Nealy, thank you for all of your critiques, patience, and dinners —DR

Millbrook Press
A division of Lerner Publishing Group, Inc.
241 First Avenue North
Minneapolis, MN 55401 U.S.A.

Website address: www.lernerbooks.com

The images in this book are used with the permission of:
© Ladi Kern/Alamy, p. 32; Library of Congress (LC-DIG-cwpb-06437), p. 33.

Library of Congress Cataloging-in-Publication Data

Figley, Marty Rhodes, 1948-
President Lincoln, Willie Kettles, and the telegraph machine / by Marty Rhodes Figley ; illustrated by David Riley.
p. cm. — (History speaks: picture books plus reader's theater)
Includes bibliographical references.
ISBN 978-1-58013-671-6 (lib. bdg. : alk. paper)
1. Lincoln, Abraham, 1809-1865—Juvenile literature. 2. Telegraph—United States—History—19th century—Juvenile literature. 3. United States—History—Civil War, 1861-1865—Communications—Juvenile literature. 4. Lincoln, Abraham, 1809-1865—Military leadership—Juvenile literature. I. Riley, David, 1977- ill. II. Title.
E457.45.F54 2011
973.7092—dc22 2009050062

Manufactured in the United States of America
1 - BP - 7/15/10

CONTENTS

WASHINGTON CITY (NOW WASHINGTON, D.C.)

Tuesday, March 7, 1865

Tap! Tap-tap! Tap-tap-tap! Willie Kettles tapped his fork against the plate.

Mrs. Paul smiled at him as she cleared the breakfast dishes.

"Ah, Willie," she said. "Caught you sending telegraph messages on my china again!"

Willie laughed at Mrs. Paul's gentle teasing. She knew that you couldn't send a real telegraph message without a telegraph machine.

Fifteen-year-old Willie was a telegraph expert. He sent and received messages for the U.S. Military Telegraph Corps. He was their youngest operator.

"You better be off, or you'll be late!" Mrs. Paul said.

Willie grabbed his jacket and cap. "Thanks for the tasty biscuits!" he called.

Willie rushed out of Mrs. Paul's boardinghouse, where he lived. Washington City was already bustling. Wagons and carriages crowded Pennsylvania Avenue. Hotels, restaurants, and stores were open for business, even though the nation was at war. The Civil War between the Northern and Southern states had been going on for four years.

Willie still thought of Washington City as the capital of the whole nation. But he knew that eleven Southern states did not think of it that way. They had their own capital in Richmond, Virginia. Richmond was only ninety miles away.

For almost a year, Union armies of the North had been battling their way toward Richmond. General Ulysses S. Grant was in command. Many people believed that if the Union soldiers captured Richmond, the war would soon be over. Willie wondered what would happen then.

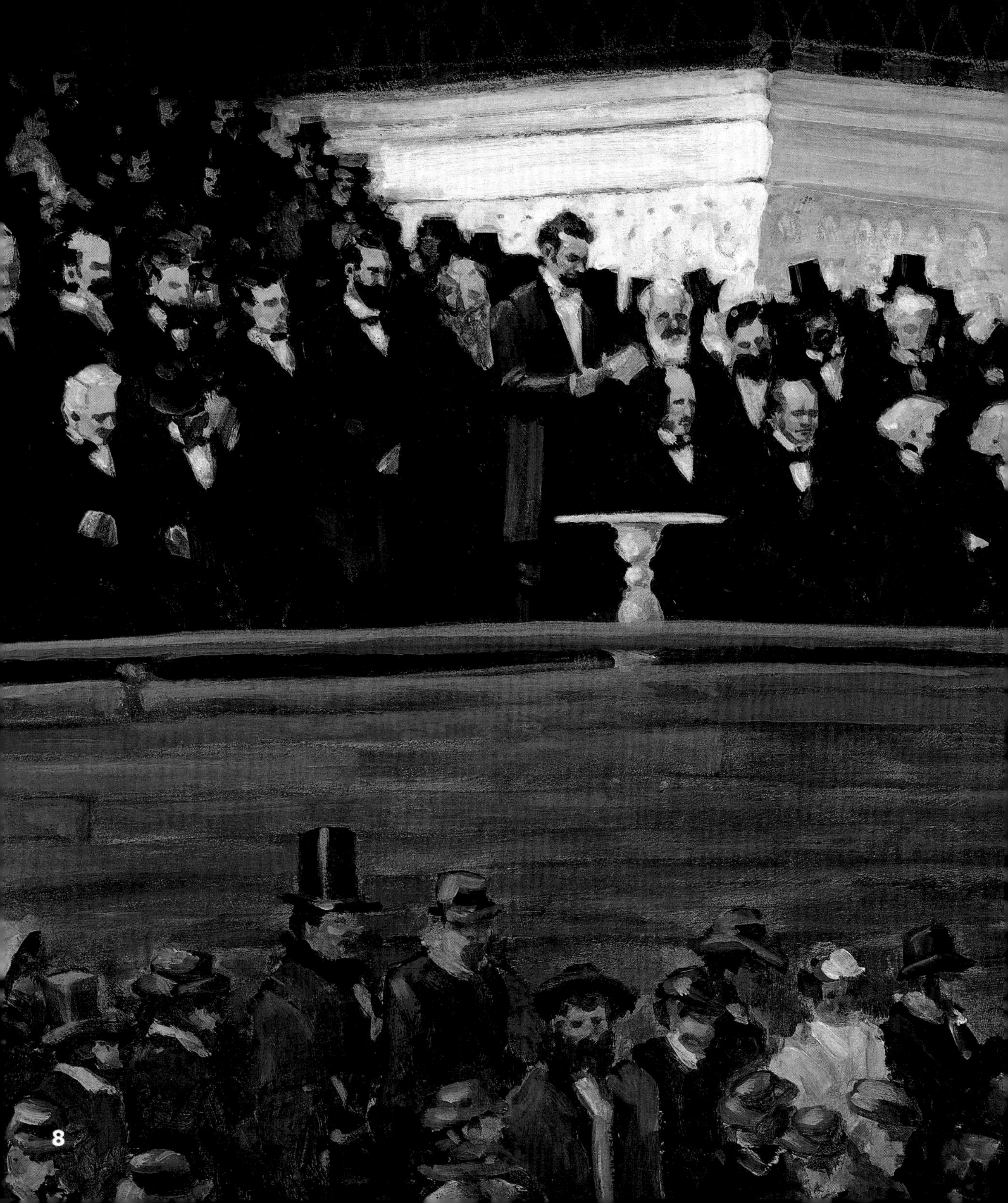

The previous Saturday, Willie had heard President Lincoln talk about the end of the war. The president was giving a speech for the beginning of his second term in office. He spoke of forgiveness. If the Southern states gave up the war, President Lincoln promised the nation would welcome them back. "With malice towards none, with charity for all," he had said.

Willie wished he could do more to help end the war. But he knew that his job was important too. He helped President Lincoln keep track of how the Union army was doing.

Willie began walking faster. He wanted to be on time. In just a few minutes, he arrived at the War Department building. Willie ran up the stairs to the second floor, where the telegraph offices were located.

As usual, the telegraph room was busy. The telegraph machines tap-tap-tapped out their electronic messages.

Homer Bates, the office manager, smiled and waved at Willie. Willie sat down at his desk. A message clicked on the telegraph machine. It was from General Grant's headquarters in City Point, Virginia. The message included some words that Willie didn't know.

The telegraph room used to be a library. A corner shelf held lots of books. The telegraph operators used an old dictionary to check spelling and definitions.

Willie meant to look up the words he didn't know in the dictionary. Instead, he opened the tall book leaning beside it. Willie thought he would just take a quick look at its colorful paintings of birds.

An angry voice said, "Come to my office, young man!"

Willie swallowed hard. It was the secretary of war, Edwin Stanton. He was strict but fair. He didn't ask anything of the workers that he didn't expect of himself.

Secretary Stanton sat down behind his desk. He took off his glasses and stared at Willie.

"May I remind you there's a war going on?" he said. Secretary Stanton pointed a finger at Willie. "You must stay at your desk!" he said. "Lack of attention in the telegraph office may cause an important message to be missed!"

"Yes, sir," Willie said. He felt his face grow hot.

There was a knock at the door.

"Come in," said Secretary Stanton.

President Lincoln walked into the room. A worn black suit fit loosely on his long, thin body.

"Good morning, gentlemen," he said. He looked from Willie to Secretary Stanton.

Secretary Stanton was still frowning at Willie. President Lincoln leaned over and ruffled Willie's hair. Willie thought he had the kindest and saddest eyes he had ever seen.

"On my way over, I heard a newsboy calling out for people to buy a newspaper," said President Lincoln. "That reminded me of a funny story."

President Lincoln smiled at Willie. He said, "Several years ago, I had a bad photograph taken with my hair all tousled. When the newspaper boys sold the paper with this picture in it, they yelled, 'Here's your Old Abe. He'll look better when he gets his hair combed!'"

Secretary Stanton laughed. The president winked at Willie.

Secretary Stanton said to Willie, "It's back to work for you, my lad."

The two men followed Willie back to the telegraph room. The president checked the drawer that held the latest telegraph messages.

Willie admired the way the president used the telegraph to lead the war. He communicated quickly with the generals on the battlefield. President Lincoln called the telegraph messages "lightning messages."

The president visited the War Department at least twice a day. Often he worked late into the evening. When waiting for news of important battles, he spent the night. The department kept a cot there especially for him.

Willie sighed. He was still upset because Secretary Stanton had scolded him.

Willie knew he was a hard worker and smart. He wished Secretary Stanton thought so too.

In the evening, Willie returned to Mrs. Paul's boardinghouse. She took a good look at him. "Why the sad face, lad?" she asked. "I've got a big piece of my blueberry pie that's been waiting for you!"

Willie's day suddenly seemed better.

Two weeks later, President Lincoln stood in the telegraph room reading a message. Willie watched as he put it down.

"I will be leaving tomorrow to visit General Grant at his headquarters," he said to Homer.

Homer nodded, "It will be good for you to have a break from all your duties here in Washington." He paused and then blurted, "But don't get too close to the battles!"

President Lincoln smiled at Homer. "I'll do my best," he said.

Willie looked out the window by his desk. He watched the president walk back across the shady lawn to the White House. President Lincoln's tall body seemed stooped. All the worries of this war must be troubling him.

"Please stay safe, sir," Willie whispered.

On April 3, Secretary Stanton entered the telegraph room. He walked past Willie without a glance. He went straight to his office and shut the door.

Willie mumbled, "And a good morning to you too, sir."

Around noon, a telegraph message came clacking across the Fort Monroe, Virginia, line. It said, *"Turn down for Richmond, quick!"*

Everyone stopped working, and the room went silent. There had been no messages from Richmond since the war began. The operator, Thomas Laird, adjusted the receiving instrument. Now the weaker signal could come in more clearly from Richmond

Thomas pushed Willie over to the telegraph machine.

"Here, Willie, take the message," he said. "It's from Richmond! I'll go tell Secretary Stanton it's coming!"

Willie took over the telegraph machine with shaking fingers.

Another message was clicking, *"Do you get me well?"*

Willie tapped, "I do. Go ahead!"

Then came another series of clacks: *"All right. Here's the first*

The other operators surrounded Willie. He started copying the message.

"To Secretary Stanton, Secretary of War: We entered Richmond at 8 o'clock this morning. . . . "

The operators cheered. Richmond had been captured by Union troops!

Willie finished copying the message. Then he jumped up from his chair. In his haste, he knocked over the inkstand and his telegraph instrument.

An operator leaned out the window. He yelled, "Richmond has fallen!"

A crowd gathered on the street.

Secretary Stanton rushed into the room. Willie tried to clean up the mess he had made. Secretary Stanton didn't seem to mind. He patted Willie on the back and said, "Good job, lad!" Then he went over to the window and waved at the crowd.

Before Willie could gather his senses, Stanton whisked him over to the window.

"This is the boy who took the important message!" he said.

The crowd yelled, "Speech, speech!"

Willie was too tongue-tied to say anything. But he felt about ten feet tall.

President Lincoln was still with General Grant. Willie wished the president were here with them celebrating. But he knew this important lightning message would quickly reach President Lincoln.

Willie hoped that now that Richmond had fallen, the war would soon end. Then the country could come

Afterword

A TELEGRAPH MACHINE

In 1844, inventor Samuel Morse sent the first telegraph message. It went from Washington to Baltimore, Maryland. By 1861, telegraph lines crisscrossed the United States. They ran along railroad tracks.

Abraham Lincoln was the first U.S. president to use the telegraph to fight a war. The telegraph lines were connected to the War Department building. President Lincoln spent many hours at the War Department telegraph office. He was friendly with young telegraph operators who worked there. President Lincoln sometimes used humor to relax people. The joke Lincoln shared with Willie and Secretary Stanton is one that he actually told.

Willie Kettles was a real telegraph operator. Operators around Willie's age often ran early telegraph offices. Many teenage telegraphers worked on the battlefields. They sent and received messages about the battles on portable telegraph machines.

SECRETARY OF WAR EDWIN M. STANTON

The story about the important message from Richmond and Willie's role in receiving it is true. After Richmond fell, the war soon came to an end. On April 9, 1865, General Robert E. Lee, the head of the Confederate army, surrendered to General Ulysses S. Grant at Appomattox Court House in Virginia.

Celebrations were cut short. John Wilkes Booth, a Southern supporter, shot President Lincoln as he watched a play at Ford's Theatre on April 14, 1865. President Lincoln died the next day. Both the North and South suffered at the loss of this great, kind leader.

Performing Reader's Theater

Dear Student,
Reader's Theater is a dramatic reading. It is a little like a play, but you don't need to memorize your lines. Here are some tips that will help you do your best in a Reader's Theater performance.

BEFORE THE PERFORMANCE

- **Choose your part:** Your teacher may assign parts, or you may be allowed to choose your own part. The character you play does not need to be the same age as you. A boy can play the part of a girl, and a girl can play the part of a boy. That's why it's called acting!
- **Find your lines:** Your character's name is always the same color. The name at the bottom of each page tells you which character has the first line on the next page. If you are allowed to write on your script, highlight your lines. If you cannot write on the script, you may want to use sticky flags to mark your lines.
- **Check pronunciations of words:** If your character's lines include any words you aren't sure how to pronounce, check the pronunciation guide on page 45. If a word isn't there or you still aren't sure how to say it, check a dictionary or ask a teacher, librarian, or other adult.
- **Use your emotions:** Think about how your character feels in the story. If you imagine how your character feels, the audience will hear the emotion in your voice.
- **Use your imagination:** Think about how your character's voice might sound. For example, an old man's voice will sound different from a baby's voice. If you do change your voice, make sure the audience can still understand the words you are saying.

- **Practice your lines:** Even though you do not need to memorize your lines, you should still be comfortable reading them. Read your lines aloud often so they flow smoothly.

DURING THE PERFORMANCE

- **Keep your script away from your face but high enough to read:** If you cover your face with your script, you block your voice from the audience. If you have your script too low, you need to tip your head down farther to read it and the audience won't be able to hear you.
- **Use eye contact:** Good Reader's Theater performers look at the audience as much as they look at their scripts. If you look down, the sound of your voice goes down to the script and not out to the audience.
- **Speak clearly:** Make sure you are loud enough. Say all your words carefully. Be sure not to read too quickly. Remember, if you feel nervous, you may start to speak faster than usual.
- **Use facial expressions and gestures:** Your facial expressions and gestures (hand movements) help the audience know how your character is feeling. If your character is happy, smile. If your character is angry, cross your arms and be sure not to smile.
- **Have fun:** It's okay if you feel nervous. If you make a mistake, just try to relax and keep going. Reader's Theater is meant to be fun for the actors and the audience!

Cast of Characters

NARRATOR 1

NARRATOR 2

WILLIE KETTLES:
a fifteen-year-old boy

EDWIN STANTON:
U.S. secretary of war

ABRAHAM LINCOLN:
President of the United States

READER 1:
Mrs. Paul, telegraph messages

READER 2:
Homer Bates (office manager),
Thomas Laird (telegraph operator)

ALL:
Everyone except sound

SOUND:
This part has no lines. The person in this role
is in charge of the sound effects.
Find the sound effects for this script
at www.historyspeaksbooks.com.

The Script

NARRATOR 1: In 1865, Willie Kettles was fifteen years old. He lived in Washington City. In modern times, we call this city Washington, D.C.

SOUND: [silverware tapping]

NARRATOR 2: Willie tapped his fork against his plate. Mrs. Paul smiled at him as she cleared the breakfast dishes.

READER 1 (AS MRS. PAUL): Ah, Willie. Caught you sending telegraph messages on my china again!

NARRATOR 1: Willie laughed. He was a telegraph expert. He sent and received messages for the U.S. Military Telegraph Corps. He was their youngest operator.

NARRATOR 2: Operators around Willie's age often ran early telegraph offices. Telegraphers sent and received messages on telegraph machines.

READER 1 (AS MRS. PAUL): You better be off, or you'll be late!

WILLIE: Thanks for the biscuits, Mrs. Paul!

NARRATOR 1: Willie rushed out the door of Mrs. Paul's boardinghouse. Washington City was already bustling. Hotels, restaurants, and stores were open for business, even though the nation was at war.

NARRATOR 2: The Civil War between the Northern and Southern states had been going on for four years.

Next Page — **NARRATOR 1**

NARRATOR 1: Willie thought of Washington City as the capital of the entire nation. But he knew that eleven Southern states did not think of it that way. They had their own capital in Richmond, Virginia.

NARRATOR 2: For almost a year, the Union army of the North had been battling its way toward Richmond. General Ulysses S. Grant was in command. Many people believed that if the Union soldiers captured Richmond, the war would soon be over.

NARRATOR 1: The past Saturday, Willie had heard President Lincoln talk about the end of the war. The president spoke of forgiveness. If the Southern states gave up the war, President Lincoln promised the nation would welcome them back.

LINCOLN: With malice towards none, with charity for all.

WILLIE: I wish I could do more to help end the war. But I do help President Lincoln keep track of how the Union army is doing.

NARRATOR 2: Abraham Lincoln was the first U.S. president to use the telegraph to fight a war. The telegraph lines were connected to the War Department building, where President Lincoln spent many hours.

NARRATOR 1: In just a few minutes, Willie arrived at the War Department building. He ran up the stairs to the telegraph offices. The telegraph room was busy. Machines tap-tap-tapped out their electronic messages.

SOUND: [telegraph machine tapping]

Next Page — **NARRATOR 2**

NARRATOR 2: Homer Bates, the office manager, smiled and waved at Willie. Willie sat down at his desk. A message clicked on the telegraph machine. It was from General Grant's headquarters in City Point, Virginia. The message included some words that Willie didn't know.

NARRATOR 1: The telegraph operators used an old dictionary to check spelling and definitions. Willie meant to look up the words he didn't know in the dictionary. Instead, he opened the tall book leaning beside it. Willie thought he would just take a moment to look at its colorful paintings of birds.

STANTON: Come to my office, young man!

NARRATOR 2: It was the secretary of war, Edwin Stanton. He was strict but fair. He didn't ask anything of the workers that he didn't expect of himself. Secretary Stanton sat down behind his desk. He took off his glasses and stared at Willie.

STANTON: May I remind you there's a war going on? You must stay at your desk! Lack of attention in the telegraph office may cause an important message to be missed!

WILLIE: Yes, sir.

SOUND: [knock on door]

STANTON: Come in.

NARRATOR 1: President Lincoln walked into the room. A worn black suit fit loosely on his long, thin body.

Next Page — **LINCOLN**

LINCOLN: Good morning, gentlemen.

NARRATOR 2: Lincoln looked from Willie to Secretary Stanton. Secretary Stanton was still frowning at Willie. President Lincoln leaned over and ruffled Willie's hair. Willie thought he had the kindest and saddest eyes he had ever seen.

LINCOLN: On my way over, I heard a newsboy calling out for people to buy a newspaper. That reminded me of a funny story. Several years ago, I had a bad photograph taken with my hair all tousled. When the newspaper boys sold the paper with this picture in it, they yelled, "Here's your Old Abe. He'll look better when he gets his hair combed!"

NARRATOR 1: Secretary Stanton laughed. The president winked at Willie. President Lincoln used humor to put people at ease.

STANTON: It's back to work for you, my lad.

NARRATOR 2: President Lincoln and Secretary Stanton followed Willie back to the telegraph room. The president checked the latest telegraph messages. Willie admired the way the president used the telegraph to lead the war and communicate with the generals on the battlefield. President Lincoln called the telegraph messages "lightning messages."

NARRATOR 1: The president visited the War Department at least twice a day. Often he worked late into the evening. When waiting for news of important battles, he spent the night. The department kept a cot there especially for him.

Next Page — **WILLIE**

WILLIE: I'm still upset. I know I'm a hard worker and smart! I wish Secretary Stanton thought so too.

NARRATOR 2: In the evening, Willie returned to Mrs. Paul's boardinghouse. She took a good look at him.

READER 1 (AS MRS. PAUL): Why the sad face, lad? I've got a big piece of my blueberry pie that's been waiting for you!

NARRATOR 2: Willie's day suddenly seemed better.

NARRATOR 1: Two weeks later, President Lincoln stood in the telegraph room next to Homer Bates, the office manager. Willie watched as he reviewed a message.

LINCOLN: I will be leaving tomorrow to visit General Grant at his headquarters.

READER 2 (AS BATES): It will be good for you to have a break from all your duties here in Washington. But don't get too close to the battles!

LINCOLN: I'll do my best.

NARRATOR 2: Willie looked out the window by his desk. He watched the president walk back across the shady lawn to the White House. President Lincoln's tall figure seemed bent down.

WILLIE: All the worries of this war must be troubling him. Please stay safe, sir!

NARRATOR 1: On April 3, Secretary Stanton entered the telegraph room and walked past Willie without a glance. He went straight to his office and shut the door.

Next Page — **WILLIE**

WILLIE: And a good morning to you too, sir.

NARRATOR 2: Around noon, a telegraph message came clacking across the Fort Monroe, Virginia, line.

READER 1 (READING MESSAGE): Turn down for Richmond, quick!

NARRATOR 1: Everyone stopped working, and the room went silent. There had been no messages from Richmond since the war began. The operator, Thomas Laird, adjusted the receiving instrument. Now the weaker signal could come in more clearly from Richmond. Thomas pushed Willie over to the telegraph machine.

READER 2 (AS LAIRD): Here, Willie, take the message. It's from Richmond! I'll go tell Secretary Stanton it's coming!

NARRATOR 2: Willie took over the telegraph machine with shaking fingers. Another message was clicking.

READER 1 (READING MESSAGE): Do you get me well?

NARRATOR 1: Willie tapped back.

WILLIE: I do. Go ahead!

NARRATOR 1: Then came another series of clacks.

READER 1 (READING MESSAGE): All right. Here's the first message for you in four years.

NARRATOR 1: The other operators in the room gathered around Willie. He started copying the message.

Next Page — **READER 1**

READER 1 (READING MESSAGE): To Secretary Stanton, Secretary of War: We entered Richmond at 8 o'clock this morning. . . .

NARRATOR 2: The operators cheered. Richmond had been captured by Union troops! Willie finished copying the message. Then he jumped up from his chair. In his haste, he knocked over the inkstand and his telegraph instrument. An operator leaned out of the window and yelled.

READER 2 (AS OPERATOR): Richmond has fallen!

SOUND: [crowd cheering]

NARRATOR 1: A crowd quickly gathered on the street. Secretary Stanton rushed into the room. Willie scrambled to clean up the mess he had made. But Secretary Stanton didn't seem to mind. He patted Willie on the back.

STANTON: Good job, lad!

NARRATOR 2: Stanton strode over to the window and waved at the crowd. Before Willie could gather his senses, Stanton whisked him over to the window.

STANTON: This is the boy who took the important message!

ALL: Speech, speech!

NARRATOR 1: Willie was too tongue-tied to say anything. But he felt about ten feet tall.

Next Page — **NARRATOR 2**

NARRATOR 2: President Lincoln was still with General Grant. Willie wished the president were here with them celebrating. But he knew this important lightning message would quickly reach President Lincoln. Willie hoped that now that Richmond had fallen, the war would soon end. Then the country could come together again.

ALL: The End

Pronunciation Guide

telegraph: TEL-uh-graf
telegrapher: tuh-LEG-gruh-fer

Glossary

City Point, Virginia: a town in Virginia located 112 miles from Washington, D.C. It was General Grant's headquarters from 1864 to 1865. (It's part of Hopewell, Virginia.)

Confederate States of America: eleven Southern states that tried to leave the United States in 1861, leading to the Civil War. They acted as an independent country until their defeat in 1865.

Morse code: a telegraph code in which letters and numbers are represented by a series of dots and dashes (short and long signals)

newsboy: a boy who sells newspapers

secretary of war: head of the War Department

telegram: the message taken and written down by the telegraph operator

telegrapher: a person who operates and takes messages from a telegraph machine

telegraph machine: a machine used to communicate at a distance using electrical signals traveling across wire (usually in Morse code)

Union: those states that remained loyal to the United States during the Civil War

War Department: the department in the government that was in charge of the military forces, along with the president. The president was (and still is) commander-in-chief. It is now called the Department of Defense.

Selected Bibliography

Bates, David Homer. *Lincoln in the Telegraph Office: Recollections of the United States Military Telegraph Corps during the Civil War.* 1907. Reprint, Lincoln: University of Nebraska Press, 1995.

Brooks, Noah. *Lincoln Observed.* Edited by Michael Burlingame. Baltimore: Johns Hopkins University Press, 1998.

Coe, Lewis. *The Telegraph: A History of Morse's Invention and the Predecessors in the United States.* Jefferson, NC: McFarland & Company, 1993.

Johnston, William John. *Telegraphic Tales and Telegraphic History.* New York: William Johnston Publishers, 1890.

Markle, Donald E. *The Telegraph Goes to War.* Hamilton, NY: Edmonston Publishing, 2003.

Oates, Stephen B. *With Malice Towards None: A Life of Abraham Lincoln.* New York: HarperPerrenial, 1977.

Plum, William R. *The Military Telegraph during the Civil War in the United States.* 2 vols. 1881. Reprint, North Stratford, NH: Ayer Company, 2000.

Wheeler, Tom. *Mr. Lincoln's T-Mails. The Untold Story of How Abraham Lincoln Used the Telegraph to Win the Civil War.* New York: Collins, 2006.

Further Reading and Websites

Books

Janeczko, Paul B. *Top Secret: A Handbook of Codes, Ciphers, and Secret Writing.* Cambridge, MA: Candlewick Press, 2004.
Read this book to learn more about codes as well as ciphers. It even includes a recipe for making invisible ink.

Ransom, Candice. *Willie McLean and the Civil War Surrender.* Minneapolis: Millbrook Press, 2005.
Learn about the end of the Civil War from the perspective of Willie McLean, an eleven-year-old boy who lives in Appomattox, Virginia.

Schott, Jane A. *Abraham Lincoln.* Minneapolis: Lerner Publications Company, 2003.
This biography of Abraham Lincoln gives an overview of his life and major accomplishments.

Stanchack, John. *Civil War.* New York: Dorling Kindersley, 2000.
Check out this illustrated history of the Civil War to see photographs of the sites, people, and artifacts connected with the war.

Websites:

BrainPOP—Civil War
http://www.brainpop.com/socialstudies/freemovies/civilwar/
Watch a short movie about the Civil War, take a quiz, and check out a timeline, an experiment, and other activities.

Presidential Inaugurations
http://lcweb2.loc.gov/ammem/pihtml/pi022.html
Look at a photograph of what Willie Kettles and others saw at President Lincoln's second presidential inauguration on March 4, 1865. (Click on a photo, and then click on "JPEG version" to make it larger.)

1728 Software Morse Code
http://www.1728.com/morstest.htm
This site explains Morse code and shows how to learn it.

Dear Teachers and Librarians,

Congratulations on bringing Reader's Theater to your students! Reader's Theater is an excellent way for your students to develop their reading fluency. Phrasing and inflection, two important reading skills, are at the heart of Reader's Theater. Students also develop public speaking skills such as volume, pacing, and facial expression.

The traditional format of Reader's Theater is very simple. There really is no right or wrong way to do it. By following these few tips, you and your students will be ready to explore the world of Reader's Theater.

EQUIPMENT

Location: A theater or gymnasium is a fine place for a Reader's Theater performance, but staging the performance in the classroom works well too.

Scripts: Each reader will need a copy of the script. Scripts that are individually printed should be bound into binders that allow the readers to turn the pages easily. Printable scripts for all the books in this series are available at www.historyspeaksbooks.com.

Music Stands: Music stands are very helpful for the readers to set their scripts on.

Costumes: Traditional Reader's Theater does not use costumes. Dressing uniformly, such as all wearing the same color shirt, will give a group a polished look. Specific costume pieces can be used when a reader is performing multiple roles. They help the audience follow the story.

Props: Props are optional. If necessary, readers may mime or gesture to convey objects that are important to the story. Props can be used much like a costume piece to identify different characters performed by one reader. Prop suggestions for each story are available at www.historyspeaksbooks.com.

Background and Sound Effects: These aren't essential, but they can add to the fun of Reader's Theater. Customized backgrounds for each story in this series and sound effects corresponding to the scripts are available at www.historyspeaksbooks.com. You will need a screen or electronic whiteboard for the background. You will need a computer with speakers to play the sound effects.

PERFORMANCE

Staging: Readers usually face the audience in a straight line or a semicircle. If the readers are using music stands, the stands should be raised chest high. A stand should not block a reader's mouth or face, but it should allow for the reader to read without looking down too much. The main character is usually placed in the center. The narrator is on the end. In the case of multiple narrators, place one narrator on each end.

Reading: Reader's Theater scripts do not need to be memorized. However, the readers should be familiar enough with the script to maintain a fair amount of eye contact with the audience. Encourage readers to act with their voices by reading with inflection and emotion.

Blocking (stage movement): For traditional Reader's Theater, there are no blocking cues to follow. You may want to have the students turn the pages simultaneously. Some groups prefer that readers sit or turn their back to the audience when their characters are "offstage" or have left a scene. Some groups will have their readers move about the stage, script in hand, to interact with the other readers. The choice is up to you.

Overture and Curtain Call: Before the performance, a member of the group should announce the title and the author of the piece. At the end of the performance, all readers step in front of their music stands, stand in a line, grasp hands, and bow in unison.

Please visit www.historyspeaksbooks.com for printable scripts, prop suggestions, sound effects, a background image that can be projected on a screen or electronic whiteboard, a Reader's Theater teacher's guide, and reading-level information for all roles.